DANGEROUS JOBS™

SEARCH AND RESCUE
SPECIALISTS

Lissette Gonzalez

PowerKiDS
press™
New York

Published in 2008 by The Rosen Publishing Group, Inc.
29 East 21st Street, New York, NY 10010

First Edition

Editor: Jennifer Way
Book Design: Greg Tucker
Photo Researcher: Nicole Pristash

Photo Credits: Cover by JO2 Brian P. Biller, U.S. Navy; pp. 5, 9, 11, 13, 15, 17, 21 © Shutterstock.com; p. 7 by LCPL Cory Tepfenhart; p. 19 by Civil Air Patrol.

Library of Congress Cataloging-in-Publication Data

Gonzalez, Lissette, 1968–
    Search and rescue specialists / Lissette Gonzalez. — 1st ed.
        p. cm. — (Dangerous jobs)
    Includes index.
    ISBN-13: 978-1-4042-3779-7 (library binding)
    ISBN-10: 1-4042-3779-8 (library binding)
    1. Rescue work—United States—Juvenile literature. 2. Search and rescue operations—United States—Juvenile literature. I. Title.
    HV551.3.G66 2008
    363.34'81023—dc22

                                                                    2006100840

Manufactured in the United States of America

CONTENTS

WHAT IS SEARCH AND RESCUE?

When people get hurt, sick, or lost in places that are hard to reach, search and rescue workers are called to help. Their job is to save people from danger and get them to safety. Search and rescue is also known as SAR.

Many different kinds of people can do search and rescue. Fire departments, police departments, forest rangers, and the U.S. military all have search and rescue teams.

Finding and helping people in trouble can be dangerous work. Because of the danger, SAR teams must learn and practice many special skills.

4

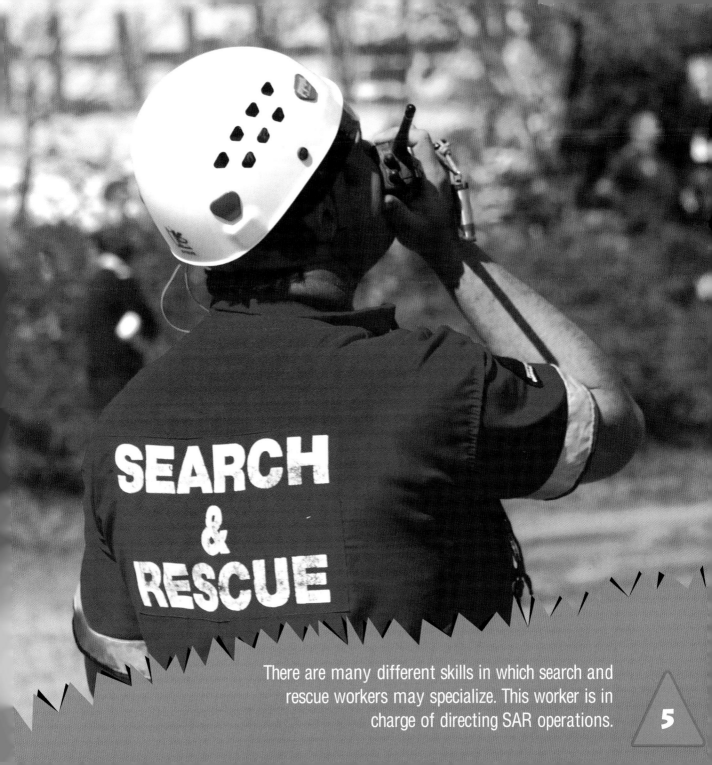

There are many different skills in which search and rescue workers may specialize. This worker is in charge of directing SAR operations.

THE SEARCH AND THE RESCUE

The first step in an SAR operation is the search. SAR workers may search on foot, on horses, or in cars. They may also search by boat, plane, or helicopter. The search may take hours or even days! Sometimes SAR teams use trained dogs. These teams are called K-9 **units**.

Once the person who needs help is found, the rescue step can begin. First the SAR team has to see if the person needs first aid. If the person is trapped, as can happen in an **earthquake** or an **avalanche**, the team tries to get the person out using its special rescue skills.

6

This Navy SAR team is using a helicopter to find and
rescue a person in a hard-to-reach location.

7

RESCUE EMTS

Some SAR units are made up of **emergency medical technicians**, or EMTs. EMTs are often the first people on the scene. Their job is to treat people who need medical attention and then to take them quickly to an emergency room.

EMTs who have SAR training are called rescue EMTs. Besides knowing how to give medical care, rescue EMTs have to know how to get people out of dangerous places, like smashed cars or caves that have **collapsed**. An EMT may need to get extra training to do these special rescue jobs.

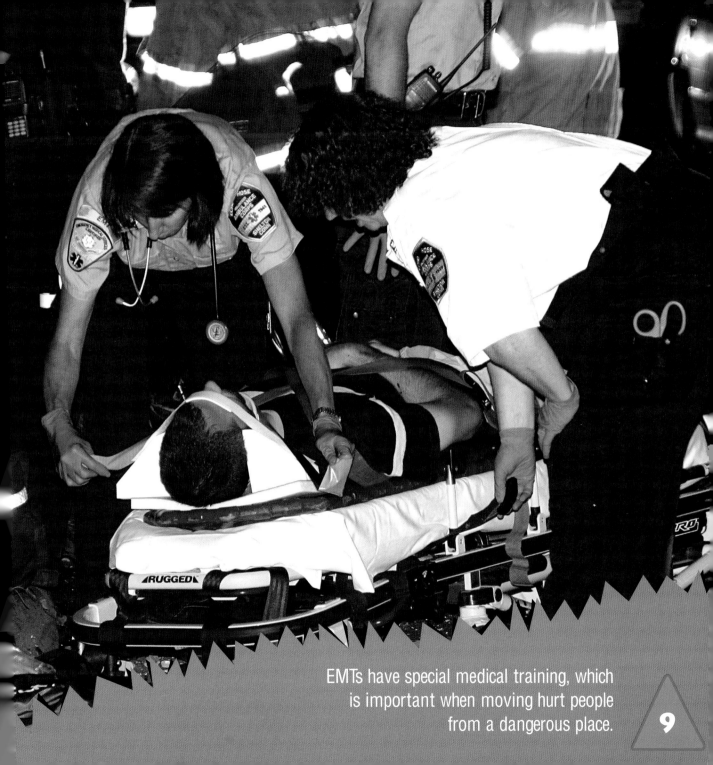

EMTs have special medical training, which
is important when moving hurt people
from a dangerous place.

9

POLICE SAR

Police officers are trained to deal with emergencies. Because of this, they can make good SAR team members. Many police departments in big cities have SAR units. Police SAR teams often take police dogs along.

Police SAR units deal with problems like **kidnapped** and missing people. They must act very quickly, before people get hurt. Because their job is to get people out of danger, people in SAR units also might get hurt.

Dogs are often a big help in SAR missions. Their sharp sense of smell and willingness to work hard make them important helpers in saving lives.

11

FIRE DEPARTMENT SAR

Firefighters are trained to find and rescue people trapped in burning buildings. Many firefighters get hurt on the job. Some even die as they try to rescue others. They may pass out from breathing smoke or get trapped where they cannot get out.

Because rescuing people from burning buildings is so dangerous, fire departments have special SAR teams whose job is to rescue firefighters trapped in burning buildings. These teams are called Rapid Intervention Teams, or RIT. The New York City Fire Department's RIT team is called the FAST. FAST stands for Firefighter Assist Search Team.

Fire SAR teams practice working through different firefighting settings so that they will be able to help people in the fastest way possible.

13

SAR AT SEA

When people need help at sea, the U.S. Coast Guard does search and rescue. The Coast Guard is part of the U.S. military. It **protects** the country's coasts and maritime waterways. "Maritime" means "something that has to do with the sea." The Coast Guard is known all around the world as a leader in the field of SAR.

When the Coast Guard gets a **distress signal** from someone at sea, it needs to act quickly. The SAR teams leave their boat and airlift stations within 30 minutes of the signal. They use fast boats and helicopters to get to people before they drown.

This is a U.S. Coast Guard boat on a rescue operation off of the California coast.

15

MOUNTAIN SAR

Mountain SAR teams may be made up of park rangers or state police, but often they are made up of **volunteers**. People who know how to climb mountains and know their way around them volunteer to be part of mountain SAR teams. Mountain SAR teams may need special **equipment**, like ropes and ice screws, to get to lost climbers.

People sometimes get lost or hurt when they are out skiing or enjoying other snow sports. When this happens, ski patrols are called to do SAR. Many ski patrollers are also trained as EMTs.

Mountain SAR teams need to learn to use special ropes and gear to get to people in dangerous mountain areas.

THE CIVIL AIR PATROL

The Civil Air Patrol is an auxiliary group of the U.S. Air Force. "Auxiliary" means "working with another group." The Civil Air Patrol is made up of civilian pilots, or people who are not in the military who fly planes. The Civil Air Patrol rescues about 100 people every year.

The Civil Air Patrol is needed for rescues in which SAR teams fly over a large area to look for plane crashes or other **accidents**. The Civil Air Patrol flies Cessna 172 Skyhawks and Cessna 182 Skylanes. However, some volunteers use their own planes when they are called on SAR missions.

This is a Civil Air Patrol Cessna airplane. The letters on the tail say that it belongs to an auxiliary unit of the U.S. Air Force.

DANGER IS THE JOB

People who do SAR put their lives in danger. When they go into dangerous places, there is a chance that they will get hurt, lost, or even killed.

For example, some of the firefighters and EMTs who went to help people at the World Trade Center on 9/11 became trapped in the falling buildings. Some rescuers died. Others were saved but were hurt or got sick from breathing in dust and smoke.

SAR people see danger as part of their job. They are brave people who understand that they must face danger so others may live.

Airlifts are one of the many dangerous
tasks that SAR workers face.

WHY BECOME AN SAR SPECIALIST?

People who work on SAR teams may do it for a living. Other people are volunteers. Volunteers are often people who know a lot about getting to dangerous places. Mountain climbers, pilots, and practiced skiers are among the many kinds of people who volunteer for SAR work.

There are many reasons that people do SAR. Some like to put their bodies and minds to the test. Others do it because they love going into dangerous places and helping others. One thing all rescuers have in common is that they enjoy helping people and saving lives.

GLOSSARY

accidents (AK-seh-dents) Unexpected and sometimes bad events.

avalanche (A-vuh-lanch) When a large amount of snow, ice, earth, or dirt slides down a mountainside.

collapsed (kuh-LAPST) Fell down or caved in.

distress signal (dih-STRES SIG-nul) A call for help from people who are in danger.

earthquake (URTH-kwayk) A shaking of Earth's surface caused by the movement of large pieces of land called plates that run into each other.

emergency medical technicians (ih-MUR-jin-see MEH-dih-kul tek-NIH-shunz) People whose job it is to take care of sick or hurt people until they can get to a hospital.

equipment (uh-KWIP-mint) All the supplies needed to do something.

kidnapped (KID-napt) To have been carried off by force.

protects (pruh-TEKTS) Keeps safe.

units (YOO-nets) Groups of people.

volunteers (vah-lun-TEERZ) People who offer to work for no money.

23

INDEX

B
boat(s), 6, 14

D
distress signal, 14
dogs, 6, 10

E
earthquake, 6
emergency medical
    technician(s) (EMTs),
    8, 16, 20
emergency room, 8

F
fire departments, 4, 12
first aid, 6
forest rangers, 4

H
helicopter(s), 6, 10, 14
horses, 6

P
plane(s), 6, 18
police departments, 4,
    10

S
safety, 4
skills, 4, 6

T
training, 8

U
unit(s), 6, 8, 10
U.S. military, 4, 14

V
volunteers, 16, 18, 22

WEB SITES

Due to the changing nature of Internet links, PowerKids Press has developed an online list of Web sites related to the subject of this book. This site is updated regularly. Please use this link to access the list:
www.powerkidslinks.com/djob/search/